The Missing Chick

For my daughter, Sasha,
and my son, Kostya
V. G.

First edition 2009

Library of Congress Cataloging-in-Publication Data is available.

Library of Congress Catalog Card Number 2008935658

ISBN 978-0-7636-3676-0

2 4 6 8 10 9 7 5 3 1

Printed in China

This book was typeset in Aunt Mildred.
The illustrations were done in ink and watercolor.

Candlewick Press
99 Dover Street
Somerville, Massachusetts 02144
visit us at www.candlewick.com

The Missing Chick

Valeri Gorbachev

CANDLEWICK PRESS

One day, Mother Hen and her chicks were hanging up the laundry.

Mrs. Duck came by. "Hello," said Mrs. Duck. "I see that everyone is busy."

"Yes," said Mother Hen. "My seven chicks are very good helpers!"

"But I only see six chicks," said Mrs. Duck.

"Maybe we forgot one at home," said Mother Hen.

She looked under the table and under the chairs.
"He's not here," said Mother Hen.

She checked all the beds. *"He's not here, either."*

"Have you seen my chick?" she asked the neighbors.
"No," they said, "but we will help you look."

Neighbor Goat looked in the bushes. *"He's not here,"* he said.

Neighbor Sheep looked in the grass. *"He's not here,"* she said.

Neighbor Pig looked under the porch. *"He's not here,"* she said.

"Where are you, little chick?" called Mrs. Duck, hopping from one foot to the other.

The police arrived.

"One of my chicks is missing!" Mother Hen said.

The police looked on the roof. They looked behind the chimney. They looked in the attic.

"*He's not here,*" they said.

The detective questioned the neighbors.

He looked for footprints.

He even talked to the little chick's brothers and sisters.
But no one had any idea where the missing chick was.

The firefighters showed up in their big red truck.

The firefighters looked in all the trees. *"He's not here,"* they said.

They looked at the bottom of all the hills.
"He's not here," they said.

The missing chick was nowhere to be found!

"Where are you, little chick?" cried Mother Hen.

"Where are you, little chick?" cried the police
officer in the helicopter.

"Where are you, little chick?" cried everyone.

"It's awful, awful, awful!" cried Mrs. Duck, running from one end of the clothesline to the other.

"Where are you, poor little chick?"

Suddenly Mrs. Duck stopped wailing.
Something had moved in the laundry basket!

It was the missing chick!

"What were you doing in there?" asked Mrs. Duck.

"I was taking a nap," said the little chick. "But it got so noisy that I woke up."

"*Here he is!*" shouted Mrs. Duck. "I found the missing chick!"

Mother Hen ran over. "You found him! You found my missing chick! Thank you! Thank you very much!"

"Hooray!" everyone cheered. "The missing chick has been found!"

"Now everything is as it should be," said Mrs. Duck.
"Don't get lost again, little chick!"

"Oh, I won't, Mrs. Duck!" said the little chick.

"I promise!"